INCUBUS BORN

A DEATH MAIDEN STORY

R.R. BORN

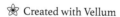

For everyone who believes in true love
&
For those of us who just likes a good party.
Cheers!
Santé!

1

AS I AM TODAY

*H*er mouth felt amazing going up and down my cock. When I'd stepped into the gentleman's club, The Kinky Rabbit, I wasn't searching for any companionship. Even if my nature dictated I should always want company, alas, I'd never been one to do the expected.

Of all the women who'd crossed my path tonight, this pink-and-white-striped-haired temptress and her best friend, Delilah, were gifts. Both women used their hands, mouths, and bodies in a seamless conflagration of pleasure. The sensations skittering up my spine made it hard to concentrate as I sucked and nipped the tips of Delilah's lightly tanned breasts. My teeth sank deep into her soft flesh.

While I could have been mistaken for a vampire, all I wanted to drain from her was unadulterated pleasure. She screamed out, but it didn't sound like a cry of pain, so I watched her friend's tongue ring flicker around my cock. It was enough to make anyone forget everything and everyone around them.

My body tightened from the sensations. I was close, but

the climax I desired was a different sort of orgasm. I pulled my mouth away from Delilah's delectable mounds, threaded my fingers through the thick mane of pink-and-white hair bobbing in my lap, and lifted the woman off. Her mouth released me with a pop, and she groaned aloud her dissatisfaction while reaching for me again. I tightened my grip and jerked her head back to look up at me. Her lips were plump, and her pupils were blown wide open as her body hummed with sexual energy, the desire dripping off her like honey. She was ready for me.

Commanding, "Kiss me," I released her, then leaned back against the headboard.

She rose to her knees on the bed, not taking her eyes off mine, and then climbed the last few inches up my chest. I ran my hand over her petite frame, between her legs, and through her folds, coating my fingers with her wetness. The moment I touched the little bud, she screamed out.

That's when I struck.

Flipping her onto her back, my lips covered hers in a fierce tangle of lips, teeth, and tongues. Her being wet wasn't enough, though. Her desiring me wasn't enough either. To feed the curse, I needed more. I needed a little piece of her soul. My lips greedily tugged at hers and pulled her tongue into my mouth as I sucked down her continued cries of pleasure. With every draw, her spiritual energy poured into me, melting on my tongue like warm chocolate, and she tasted just as sweet. With one last tug of her tongue, I released her.

She smiled, a goofy satisfied grin.

"No, fair. Stop hogging him, Azalea," Delilah whined.

I looked over, and her bottom lip was pouted out. When I leaned her way, the woman under me moaned.

"Mmm, you're so yummy. I really want another—" Azalea's mouth opened wide as she yawned.

"I think that's enough for right now." After placing a kiss on her forehead, I crawled from on top of her.

Azalea curled up and drifted off the moment I moved. It was hard to believe the fiery sex kitten from a minute ago was now asleep like a baby.

Still pouty, Delilah offered an irresistible and tempting sight. My hands went to either side of her face, right before I sucked her plump bottom lip into my mouth. She kept moving her head from side to side, trying to deepen the kiss, but that wasn't what I wanted. With playful licks and nips, I wanted to enjoy the taste of her on my tongue, the feel of her in my mouth.

Azalea had sated the curse—I wouldn't need to feed again for a while—but there was something about this woman. Perhaps it was her long black hair. Maybe it was the way she gave herself to me without hesitation. Might have even been the way she pouted—a weakness I'd yet to outgrow in my many centuries in this world.

In an effort to take over, Delilah flung her leg over my lap and ground her sex into my groin. Then using her hands to lift my mouth to hers, her tongue tangled with mine, demanding and so unlike the gentle caresses I'd just given her. I closed my eyes and let her control the kiss while opening myself enough to allow a small bit of her essence to flow through me.

Breathless, Delilah pulled back and gazed into my eyes. "Dude, has anyone ever told you that you are like, so addictive?"

"Maybe a time or two." The tip of my tongue ran along her neck. A shiver ran through her when I sucked behind her ear, lending me more spiritual energy than I needed. My well was full.

Her hands rolled over my chest. One finger kept coming back to a sensitive spot. Not a fresh wound, but an old scar. I grabbed her fingers, sucking each into my mouth, causing her to cry out. Yet, over and over, her finger kept touching the roughened flesh, making me again move her away.

The tip of her tongue licked my neck, then she kissed the same spot. Her finger touched the spot again. "What's this?"

My eyes didn't waver or look down when I responded. "That?" I pulled Delilah's fingers away again, this time holding them. The raised skin, shaped in a horizontal infinity sign, looked as perfect as the day I'd received it. "It's a sign of my undying love."

Delilah stared into my eyes with a hint of a smile. "You were in love?"

"Once."

My open palm slapped her ass. Delilah opened her mouth like she was going to ask more, but another, harder slap ensured she got the message and got off me.

I refused to talk about it. Hell, it felt wrong to think about *her* with another woman on my lap.

But it didn't matter what I didn't want to think about. Memories flooded my mind with a past I'd tried to forget. And a love that would never let me go.

2

HER

*I*t was the spring of 1710 and the first time I ever saw her. I was twenty-five and in the prime of my life. Apart from the fact that my father thought he could marry me off to any noble family to gain respectability. I wasn't looking for love and certainly not a wife. Being able to carve out a good life and a family in these changing times in France is what I wanted.

Bernard's carriage had enough bells and whistles that people often mistook it for that of royalty. But, alas, he was the son of an English marquess and a Parisian courtesan, nothing more. His father had always sent him a healthy annual living expense and pocket money, an amount which seemed like more since his mother died last year. The Marquess would never pass his title down to his French first-born bastard son because he had a legal heir in London.

Before stepping into the carriage, I instructed the driver to take us to the outskirts of our village of Valens, to the lavender fields.

"Gentlemen," I said as I got in.

Bernard and Pierre both gave me a tight nod in response.

"Toussaint, when are you going to move out of your parents' home? That can't be comfortable." Bernard leaned against the carriage window.

When I first met Bernard and Pierre at University, Bernard had declared that there were too many men named 'François' in France, let alone the school. He had a valid point and I couldn't dispute him. My friend then decided to address me by my family name.

"I don't know. Every time I bring it up, my mother seems to catch the vapors. It's easier to stay than deal with her and her tears. As long as she doesn't insist on matchmaking, I can stay a little longer."

"Amen, brother," Pierre added.

A quarter of an hour into the ride, Bernard pulled back the curtain, and looking out the window, commenting, "Where the hell is Langley taking us? He's driven us to the club hundreds of times. He's old, I know, but not senile." He reached out the window, but I stopped him before he could halt the driver.

"I told him to take us somewhere else."

Both Bernard and Pierre eyed me like I had stolen their coin.

"To that House of Venus or maybe the new Turkish bath?" Pierre inquired, smiling from ear to ear. His devilish grin belied his angelic looks.

This time, Bernard and I turned to look at Pierre.

"And what would you know about either?" Bernard chimed in with one haughty brow raised.

Pierre's cheeks went a bright shade of pink. "I know about prostitutes," he said with a sheepish grin. "I only look young, but I can assure you, I am a man."

All three of us sat in silence inside as the noisy carriage went along the road. Then, we all fell into laughter. Pierre was only a year younger than Bernard and myself, but he looked young. Not a day over ten years and four. He'd often said it was a gift and a curse many times over. He could talk his way out of anything because everyone thought he was naïve and innocent. The ladies, on the other hand, thought him adorable with his wide blue eyes and flaxen curls, much too young to corrupt, kiss, or deflower.

"We do not doubt you, ol' boy," I managed through a bout of laughter.

The carriage finally came to a stop and the door opened. Langley put the wooden step down and we all got out.

"Good lord, man, there's nothing here." Bernard turned in a circle.

There were trees all around. Lots and lots of greenery. I didn't remember it looking like this. It wasn't yet dark, but Langley understood where I'd asked him to take us. As I turned to inquire, the carriage pulled away and there they were—the lavender fields.

Tinny music played, hands clapped in rhythm, and laughter could be heard now. Fabric in shades of purple waved in the wind, leading to a huge open area in front of rows upon rows of lavender bushes. A breeze carried the light floral scent toward us.

For a quick moment, Bernard inhaled with his eyes closed. When he opened his eyes he looked at me with a curious smile. "What is this place?"

He'd traveled to many places with his mother as a child, but he hadn't yet experienced the festival. When she died, his father left him here in Valens, her birthplace, in between school sessions.

Pierre yelled out like a little kid, "The lavender festival!"

Bernard and I turned to him, saying nothing. It was all I could do to keep from laughing out loud. There was no way to miss his child-like joy at seeing this place.

Pierre pulled down his waistcoat down and cleared his throat. "I just haven't been here in a very long time, that's all." He walked toward the entrance while we followed him. "I wonder if the fortune teller is still here."

Although he'd said it more to himself, I still answered. "I'm sure she is."

Bernard chimed in after. "Maybe she'll tell you when you'll lose your—"

"Not! Another word," Pierre snapped as he spun around just as fast to stop what Bernard was about to say. Then he walked faster.

"Toussaint, tell me the truth. Why are we here?"

I closed my eyes and inhaled deep, as I had when I was a boy of ten. With a smile, I opened them. "I used to love this place as a kid. I don't know, mayhaps I am feeling nostalgic. Indulge me for an hour, would you, my friend?"

"It is quite fascinating," Bernard said as we passed a table with little wooden and ceramic trinkets. "I see the flowers and food, but where are the..."

His words trailed off as a group of young women walked past us dressed in a variety of long colored skirts. Their low-cut black-and-white blouses were even lower than those of courtesans, and every one had a different colored silk scarf tied on their heads. They must have been with the gypsy folk who visited this area every couple of years. Two girls giggled behind their hands as they looked at us.

It was then that *she* ran out after the other gypsy girls. The young woman didn't have a silk scarf holding back her long, black, wavy tresses. Which I was thankful for when she flipped her wild mane to the other side as a strong breeze came up and whipped it around. That's when her eyes met mine and I saw a hint of a smile before she looked away.

"All right, Toussaint, this might not be a waste of time after all."

My eyes followed her as the group walked down a row of lavender. I nodded, replying, "Not a waste at all."

3

KNOW YOUR PLACE

*U*ne *quinzaine.*

Two long weeks later, and the black-haired beauty from the lavender festival still occupied a considerable amount of space in my thoughts. That day, I'd rushed off in the same direction she had, but she seemed to disappear into thin air. I thanked the stars every night she hadn't vanished from my dreams too.

The city seemed to be busy this morning while I watched the world go by in front of my family's business, *DeChevalier's Boutique de Mercerie.* Elder thought adding 'boutique' to the name would make it seem more than a haberdashery. To his defense, having on-site seamstresses had made an increase in business. Most notably with mothers purchasing dresses for their daughters before the social season. Thus, my father had asked me to assist more than usual.

From across the street, a glimmer of dark hair caught my eye.

"François, you hear me?" Elder asked from behind me.

A carriage stopped, blocking my line of sight before I could see the woman's face.

"Son." Elder's annoyance seethed from the one word.

I turned to meet his frown. "Yes, sir?"

"Come help Mrs. Cassan and her daughter."

This is why I hated to accompany my father to the business. Elder dreamed of one day being part of high society. We weren't poor, but we weren't wealthy either. There was a lord in the family. Something my father aspired to and thought me the means to get him there. He made me feel like a prized bull every time he invited me to "*help someone.*" Elder made sure I assisted every matriarch from a titled family to give them time to appraise me.

It would be far more embarrassing if I refused and would cost us business, so I smiled and helped the ladies. Mrs. Cassan purchased everything I pointed out, and I was positive Lady Cassiopeia was half in love with me when they left.

"Father!" I called and walked toward the back office to tell him I wasn't doing this again, all the smiles and abating myself to these women. Upon opening the door, I couldn't believe my eyes.

"No, sir. Many apologies. But those were the correct measurements..." The young woman quavered in the corner.

Elder lifted his arm. "You dare speak back!"

I rushed to stop his hand from finding its mark, scolding, "That's enough, father."

The young seamstress let out a cry as she cowered. I could only guess by the bright red hand print blossoming on her warm beige skin, he'd already struck her once. To help calm the young woman, I squatted down to her level and waited.

"I'm sorry," she said over and over.

Finally, I extended my hand to help her up, but her eyes were trained behind me. Noting my father had her attention, I moved into her line of sight.

"All is well." I smiled when she looked at me with her red-rimmed eyes. "Come now."

Her legs buckled and I caught her by the waist, then walked her past my father and out of the room. "You go home for the day."

"What? She can't go home. I have orders," Elder barked, and her slight frame shook in my arms.

"All will be well," I whispered. "I will talk to him. Please come in at your normal time tomorrow."

"Thank you, young master."

I watched her get her things and leave. It took me a few minutes to calm down. Every time I visited the store, my father liked to show his greatness by attacking the workers with words. This was the first time I'd ever seen him use the back of his hand to assault someone, though. Oftentimes, it felt like I didn't even know this man.

It escaped me how he thought it was right to treat people this way. We were all human beings; as often I had tried to explain this to him, but he was adamant that people should know their place. Especially those who had skin the color of dirt, and therefore should be treated as such.

His lack of humanity angered me to no end, but I usually held my tongue for my mother's sake. I wasn't sure how much longer I could do this. Without saying a word, I marched out of the shop. In my haste to get away from my father, I collided with a little boy.

"Excuse me. I didn't see you."

"*Day-soe-lay, me-siour.* It was my mistake." The little, filthy, olive-complexioned boy picked up a mass of purple flowers from the ground and placed them into a small, woven arm basket.

My eye twitched at the injustice the boy had dealt to the French language, but I understood him well enough through his accent. The scent of lavender filled the air as he continued to pick up the small bunches. At once, *she* came to mind.

"What do you have there?"

"Lavender. Good for sleep." He stood to his full height, right about four feet tall.

"I'll take two bunches." I gave him a few coins and took the handful of purple flowers from his grubby hands.

The young boy smiled widely, displaying a missing front tooth. "*Ma-see bocoup, me-siour,*" he said with a bow.

His wild, wavy black locks needed to be washed but I patted it anyway. I don't know what made me do it, but he seemed like the little brother I never had. His smile spread even wider, if that were at all possible, which brought my own smile out in turn.

The boy ran past me in good spirits, no doubt spotting another customer. I lifted the fragrant flowers to my nose, which was when I heard the awful noise and knew the boy had picked the wrong person to solicit.

Smack! The sound of hand meeting flesh seemed to echo down the street. "Get away from me, you gypsy filth!"

My father's hand hung in the air, prepared for another slap if the child got up off the ground. Rushing forward, I blocked the boy from his assailant.

"Father!" I roared as sheer anger boiled out of me. I couldn't believe he'd struck the young boy. The frail-looking youth couldn't have been any older than seven or eight. "He's a child."

Still frowning down to where the boy cowered behind

me, my father spat, then looked up at me. "They shouldn't be anywhere near respectable people." He tugged his waistcoat down and brushed invisible dust off the sleeves, before stepping shoulder to shoulder with me to whisper, "You're too softhearted. Where did I go wrong?"

Deep breaths stayed me from saying something I couldn't take back. Bending down, I helped the young boy off the ground, a whirl of brown-and-black material swallowed him up even as an arm blocked me from touching the young boy. It was her.

"Stay away from him," the raven-haired beauty from the festival snapped as she wiped tears from both of the little boy's cheeks.

"I was only—"

She turned to me with hell in her eyes. "I saw what your kind was *only* doing. He's naught but a child."

Even in anger, she was exquisite. Glistening in the sunlight, her long, dark hair seemed laced with hints of blue. She paused long enough to look at me and her ebony eyes captivated me.

"I'm not a little boy," the child declared in a small voice through his hiccups belied the bold assertion. "And he's nice. Don't be mean to him."

They spoke a moment to each other in another language. Then she looked back to me without as much fury, calmer now. "I am sorry. Thank you for the kindness you showed to my younger brother."

Her French was much better than her younger sibling's, her voice carrying a rich, melodic tone. I never really paid attention to their language before, but I could listen to this woman talk all day—and then scream my name all night.

My father once told me the gypsies were a people without names, without loyalty, and without a country. But every time he said, "Gypsy," it was hurled out like a curse. The way this brother and sister interacted was just like his own family, or like any family in Valens for that matter. Nothing was different. From that moment on, I purged the awful term from my vocabulary. Like with so many other things, my father was wrong again.

While I was lost in the presence of this woman, whose name I didn't even know, people trampled the boy's flowers as they walked by. She turned to leave and my heart skipped a beat.

"Please, wait." Relief flowed through me when she turned back. "Let me pay you"—I waved at all the flattened purple flowers—"for those. It's the least I can do after my father..." My words died on my tongue while I reached inside my waistcoat.

"No, no," she said noting the small group of flowers still clutched in my hand. "We aren't looking for charity. You've done enough. Thank you."

She turned her attention downward, and her brother smiled and nodded as he spoke their language again. She spat on a slightly cleaner piece of cloth, then wiped his dirty cheeks as she shook her head. I was certain the boy was urging her to take the money, but she wasn't going to do it. With the disapproving tone, she delivered her next words, causing the boy to grimace before standing up a little straighter.

He moved to stand in front of me. "*Meer ci bo-coup, may...*" he looked to her for help.

"*Monsieur,*" she whispered.

"*Monsieur,*" he parroted, then extended his hand.

I shook it with a smile. "*Je vous en prie.*" You're welcome.

The young woman smiled and something cracked open inside of me. If I didn't say something now, she could be out of my life forever. My mouth opened and before I knew what I wanted to say, the words were out there.

"What's your name? I'm François Toussaint DeChevalier." My body tensed as I bent at the waist in a curt bow.

When I stood straight up awaiting her answer, her cheeks were lit in a faint pink. The young boy looked up between us, head moving back and forth. Although rather comical, I couldn't laugh or look away.

Her lips tightened to a thin line and my gut sank. I was sure she wasn't going to tell me. "At least tell me when I can see you again?" I asked as the surge of desperation rose within me.

With one look, two weeks ago, this woman had occupied my every thought. I needed to see her again.

Still nothing.

Beside her, the young boy must have gotten tired of waiting and straining his neck as he gave me the information I craved. "She is Lillianna."

"Drova!" Lillianna looked down, then snatched the little boy's hand. Her panicked eyes caught mine for a moment before she looked away. "Sorry, we must go."

"Tell him," Drova urged.

"No."

The brother and sister argued as she rushed them away. Then, Drova broke away to yell back through cupped hands, "We stay outside. Near the lavender...!"

Lillianna covered his mouth and dragged him down the street.

She'd covered young Drova's mouth but it was too late. I knew exactly where to find her.

4

A PROMISE

Lillianna. Such a beautiful name, much like the woman it belongs to. It tormented me how a woman I had seen twice and spoken to only once could occupy my mind so completely.

"Son? You listening to me?"

I blinked from the purple flowers in the vase near the window, but I didn't look away. "I'm sorry, father. What did you say?"

My father's hand waved up and down in front of my face, then Elder's face leaned into view, blocking my line of sight so I *had* to look at him.

"You are certainly your mother's child," he mumbled. "I said the Lavender Ball is at the end of the month. I would like for the family to go."

"Father, those things are nothing more than a marriage mart."

Elder patted me on the shoulder. "Nothing wrong with that. You are strapping a young man from good stock." He puffed out his chest.

My eye twitched at his words, but I carried on as if those words had not struck a nerve. "I think I will pass."

"Son, this is the last time we can go as a family. Your sister will be out next year and before you know it, married with a family of her own."

If he's thinking about that, then I'll probably have several attempts at matchmaking before my sister is wed. "I have been meaning to talk to you about this," I said. "I'm going to move out."

Elder stared at me as if I had sprouted another head. "Move out, why? There's no reason. Are you not comfortable here?" Before I could answer, he continued. "Your mother will be heartbroken. Do not utter a word to her."

Elder and I had different philosophies about politics, relationships, science, human rights, and religion. In reality, in all things, but I'd learned long ago to keep my opinions to myself. It never ended well for me. I kept my own counsel, followed my own path, and steered clear of his wrath. I would not have that luxury this time. I needed to move out of this house and find a way to support myself.

The parlor doors opened. "Keeping secrets from me, dear husband?"

My mother kissed Elder, then me.

"Of course not." Elder leveled a look of warning at me before bestowing a warm smile on her. "I was just explaining the merits of attending the Lavender Ball."

She clapped her hands in glee. "Oh, yes. We must all attend. I've had the tailors preparing new outfits for the occasion."

Lovely. I mentally rolled my eyes. "Well, I'm off to the club. Mother. Father. I bid you a good night."

There was nothing more to say. This was the precise reason why I needed to get out of this house. They were making decisions for me because I was still under their roof, but I'd been an adult for a while and now it was time for me to act like it.

After mounting my horse, I sat there pensive. The club held no appeal tonight. I turned my steed in the opposite direction instead and rode off into the night.

5

LILY

*M*y horse stopped and I looked around. *When did I leave town? For that matter, where am I?* I'd ridden, lost in thought and memories of Lillianna, but one glance skyward and I knew. The stars were always brighter and the air fresher in the countryside.

Dismounting, I gathered my wits about me. I took a deep breath, then exhaled. When I did it again, a light lavender scent filled my nose. Then, I heard it. A sweet angelic voice which seemed to pull at me, like a marionette on a string. I barely even noticed the soft scrapes of the tree branches as I stepped into another world.

Colorful wooden wagons were spread out around the edges of a clearing. The orange glow of the fire illuminated the center. A few couples held each other and swayed to the music, while others laid stretched out on fabric on the ground.

I stood in the shadows and listened. *Lillianna.* Her voice was like magic. A soothing balm to my bruised soul. I must not have hidden well because a small hand wrapped around my arm.

"You came!" the young boy exclaimed and pulled me into the light.

All I could do was laugh in response. I couldn't remember the last time someone was genuinely happy to see me. Lillianna had just finished her song when we walked up. Her gaze met mine and that sensation burned through me again. *What is this feeling?* I couldn't remember my body ever reacting to a woman this way before.

"Lily, Lily! Look who came," Drova said, all smiles.

Lillianna walked toward us and gave a slight nod. "I see." Her voice was softer this time. Of course, this situation was different. She didn't need to protect her little brother.

"Drova! Come here, boy," an older woman called from one of the more rundown wagons.

A small crowd now watched us with keen eyes. I straightened to my full height, not caring that they were watching me, although I felt a tad overdressed in my silk brocade overcoat and velvet pants. Lillianna followed my line of sight around the scowling crowd and then she over-exaggerated squinting back at them.

A man about my height rolled up the sleeves on his filthy shirt as he walked around us, then spat at my feet. He spoke in their language to Lillianna, all while never taking his gaze off me. I wasn't looking for a fight, but I would defend myself. As luck would have it, I didn't have to. Lillianna grabbed his ear and twisted, bringing him down to her height.

There was a collective gasp and I had the feeling more than one of them had been on the receiving end of this equalizing move. She said a few words in their language, then finished in French. Perhaps for my sake.

"Not that it is any of your business. He helped my brother today." She thrust his head away from her.

The man mumbled something under his breath to her, all while giving her the evil eye. He rubbed his ear as he stomped away and I learned a valuable lesson this night—never make Lillianna angry. It looked like it hurt.

I didn't realize my fingers caressed the outer lobe of my ear until she said, "Oh, not you too," and slapped at my hand. "Come on," Lillianna urged, then intertwined her fingers with mine, pulling me along behind her.

I'll admit the warmth inside of me overflowed at the fact that she'd taken my hand. Before leaving the area, she grabbed a lantern and a bottle from outside someone's wagon, and then we walked out of the encampment, still hand in hand.

We didn't go far, but the darkness engulfed us the moment we left the wagons. Soon, the thick trees opened up to reveal a small river.

"I didn't know this was here." I walked up to the embankment.

"It's one of the reasons we pick the area to stop. Well, this and the work."

It never occurred to me how they made their living, but it made sense. "The guy earlier...I take it I shouldn't have come?"

Lillianna set the lantern on the ground, then untied the knot in her skirt at her waist.

I spun around.

"What are you doing?"

"What are *you* doing?" I countered.

Her giggle tinkled like a bell. "It tis only an apron."

I turned back as she flicked the material in the air and spread it out on the ground. "Pasha likes to test his manliness against everyone. I have learned to not back away. Straight ahead with him"—she hit her fist against her palm

— "is the only way. You, do not give him attention. But I must admit, I am surprised to see you."

Her French wasn't perfect, but I loved the intonations of her accent. I nodded because this was all a surprise. "It was an accident, I assure you. I went for a ride to clear my head after a conversation with my father. He's…"

"I remember," she said, then spat.

The laugh bubbled out of me before I could stop it. "I see you remember him perfectly."

Lillianna held out the bottle she'd snagged earlier. The deep green, flat-bottomed bottle had two small cups attached by twine at the top. With deft hands, she untied them and handed one to me. After pulling the cork out, she poured some in my cup, then an equal amount in hers, which she lifted toward me with a toast of, "Devanos!"

"Cheers," I said at the same time.

Before I'd even taken a sip, the fruity scent hit my nose. I'd never smelled anything like it before. Bits of fruit hit my tongue: tart apples, oranges, and cherries, all in a sweet red wine.

"What is this?" I took a deeper drink of the elixir, emptying the small glass.

"Slow down," Lillianna said with a laugh. "It's my YaYa's special wine."

The drink had a mellowing effect. A heaviness settled over my bones and my body slumped back. My breathing slowed making everything in me settle. It seemed like my heart and mind found a balance and I needn't worry about anything else in life.

Oh, yes, this was some good stuff.

I wished all of life's questions could be answered as easily as picking apples from a tree or taking a sip of good wine, like in that moment.

"Now, Monsieur François, why are you really here?"

Maybe if I hadn't consumed the wine I wouldn't have opened my mouth. I looked into her chocolate brown eyes and the words fell from my lips like morning dew off leaves. I didn't remember everything I told Lillianna, but hoped my mouth stayed sealed regarding how much I desired her.

"I see," Lillianna said. "You have much on your mind. A new life is hard, but you are strong. I have confidence, you will find a way."

The soft notes of a violin filled the night air, followed by the tinny sound of a whistle, and then clapping hands. Without thinking about it, my foot kept pace with the tune.

"This music. I like it." It spoke to my soul. This place had a way of lightening it.

"There you are," Drova's voice called out from the darkness. When he'd reached the edge of the ring of lantern light, he stood watching us both. "What are you two doing out here?"

My muddled brain couldn't gather the words for an answer, so I looked to Lillianna, beseeching her with my eyes to answer.

"Drova, what do you want?"

"We're having a good time. I want him to join us."

"You should be in bed," she chided.

"Not tonight. Come." Drova grabbed me by the arm as he said something to Lillianna in their language, then looked back at me. "Up, up."

"You should go. He's not going to stop until you do." Lillianna took the small cup from my hands before I got up.

The entire world turned on its axis.

Or was that me?

Both of my hands flew out, palms down, as if that would

keep me level. I closed my eyes to stop the world from swaying.

One. Two. Three. I counted silently.

When I opened my eyes again, I let out a slow breath until the world righted itself and I felt a bit steadier. A hearty laugh bubbled out of me. I couldn't help it. It had been a long time since I'd felt this level of contentment.

6

CHANGE OF PLANS

*H*ours turned into days, days into weeks, and weeks into I can't see myself without this woman in my life. My fingers burned to give her the ring hidden in the silk pouch I held close to my heart. I was almost to the door when I heard my father call out.

"Oh, no, son. Not tonight." Elder grasped my shoulder. "Where have you been going every night? I haven't seen you."

Elder positioned himself in the sitting room and waited. I had no intention of answering him, but I looked him over. New shoes, a shave, and a haircut. Even a new outfit. No doubt this had all cost him a gold coin or two. It made me wonder who he was trying to impress this time.

"You going somewhere?" I pressed.

"Yes, and so are you, or did you forget?"

I was trying to understand what he was talking about when the door opened, and my mother walked in, adorned in a dress which complimented my father's new attire.

"Darling, why aren't you dressed yet? Did you not see the clothes I had Isabella put out for you?" Mother asked.

She must have read the confused look on my face. "Oh, François," she chided. "The Lavender Ball."

Ah, yes, the ball. So much had happened since we'd discussed attending it. Father had ordered me to attend, but I'd already known when he brought it up that I had no intention of going.

"About that—"

"No." Mother shook her head before I could finish the first sentence. "I will not hear of it, young man."

"Mothe—"

Her tone made me feel like a young lad as she cut me off once again. "No, this is quite important to your father and me. Your sister is already dressed. Now, go get ready. We *will* arrive as a family. You can do whatever you want after we pay our respects." She pushed me out of the parlor and toward the stairs.

There was nothing I could say when Mother got like this. She had a quiet but unshakeable determination. This was the last time I would go to one of these events. I am only doing this for my mother. I know what my father wanted this night but I could not allow that to come to pass. My heart belonged to another and always would.

My plans to see Lily tonight disappeared before my eyes. I didn't have a way to get word to her and dared not send a note with anyone from the house out to the lavender fields. The servant would certainly tell Elder. What I wanted to ask Lillianna could keep one more day.

With any luck, maybe I'd get a chance to sneak away from the ball without anyone noticing.

7

THE LAVENDER BALL

$\mathcal{I}$t had been foolish of me to think the event would be at the assembly hall like it had been years prior. This time it was held at my cousin's small estate just outside of town.

How did I not know this? Probably because you had no desire or inclination to be present tonight.

As I walked around, it seemed all of Valens was in attendance. The place reminded me of a grander version of the paintings of carnivals. A steady drum beat echoed in the distance, making the entire experience seem a little more exotic.

Now I understood why Mother had dressed us in these hideous bright crimson and gold brocade outfits. People lined the halls inside near the ballroom, but most of the crowd was outside in the garden. Colorful fabrics flowed in the breeze. In a small way, the surroundings reminded me of Lily's encampment.

God, I missed her right now. I would've loved to be anywhere but here. Moreover, I wanted to be where she was.

In the middle of the ballroom, groups of ladies and men performed a courtly dance. Moving in unison, they wove in and out of a long line, then broke off into small circles of four people each. Then rotated with their hands close, but never touching, in the center of their group, and then slid back into the long lines. Bow to your partner and all of that.

It resembled a wedding processional too much for my liking. Unless I was partnering with Lily, I had no interest in such antics. Before I could escape, a delicate voice called from behind me, "Cousin."

Only my cousin's wife called me by that title. I turned around to see her flowy iridescent gown was only outshone by her ethereal beauty. Lady Marie embodied the very essence of a fairy tonight. She approached with outstretched arms and kissed me on both cheeks. Although she was French, Marie had been raised in England.

"So good of you to make it."

"I wouldn't have missed it."

She glanced around then back to me, eyes gleaming. "It 'tis a glorious evening, is it not?"

Gazing over the crush of people and the decorations, I nodded. "It is, indeed. I'm happy I came, but I must admit" —I looked away sheepishly before admitting—"I forgot."

Lady Marie gasped with faux horror. "Sincerely you jest."

We both laughed, then she said, "You're in luck. I found the most interesting entertainment. You must go to the garden."

A young female servant chose that moment to walk up and whispered in her ear. Lady Marie nodded, then whispered something back before the young girl gave a curtsy and walked away.

"Is everything well?"

Lady Marie patted my arm. "Yes. Last minute preparations. Um, go out, enjoy yourself, but be sure to come back inside in about an hour. We are going to make an important announcement."

She was being enigmatic and I doubted any proclamation could matter half as much to me as being with Lily. I had hoped to slip away before they'd reached the climax of the evening, which now seemed unlikely to happen. But I somehow managed to plaster on a smile. "Wouldn't miss it."

"We can't do it without you." She gave me a *"you know what I mean"* smile and touched the side of her nose.

I had no idea what she was referring to, but before I could inquire any further, a group of women whisked Lady Marie away in a flurry of gauze and sheer fabrics. Her vagueness made me a little uneasy, but then, I didn't understand half of what went through women's heads.

Walking past the refreshment table, I popped a sweet petit four into my mouth. Many years ago, I learned not to linger in this area. I nodded and smiled, out of politeness, but avoided any actual eye contact. Mothers were always on the hunt to snare husbands for their daughters, after all.

They had transformed the garden into a tropical wonderland—even the topiaries and statues had swathes of colored fabric draped about them. As I cleared the stairs, looking around for a way out, I heard someone call my name.

"Mey-sueir François."

Drova walked my way with a silver tray in one hand as he waved with the other. He wore a clean pair of dark trousers, multi-colored patch vest, and a white shirt. Knowing the boy, it wouldn't take him long to get dirty.

"What are you doing here?"

He lifted the silver tray with a formal bow. "Working," Drova whispered. He seemed so proud of his job.

I couldn't keep the smile off my face.

The little boy cleared his throat before saying, "Meee lord, welcome to the Lavender Ball extravaga-extrav... extra." He took a deep breath, then resumed. "There are many special places all around." He waved a hand around his head. "Shall I take you to the Mistress of Fortune?" Drova winked, then whispered with a cupped hand, "It 'tis only YaYa."

This boy had a natural happiness about him. How could I not follow him after that? Much like his sister, the child had found a way into my heart.

"Lead the way, kind sir."

As we walked, I realized I knew a lot of the entertainers: the belly dancers, bards, and the juggler. I would know that scowl anywhere.

What was his name...Patrice? No, Pasha. Then it occurred to me, if they were all here...

My heart sped up. She should be here somewhere as well. Before I could ask Drova about his sister, he'd opened a fabric flap to reveal the entrance to a small tent and winked.

"Please enter, sir."

"Thank you." I pulled a coin out of my front vest pocket and placed it in his hand with a return wink. "For all of your hard work."

The space looked larger from the inside than it did on the outside. A rich, buttery light filled the room, but for whatever reason, my eyes lingered on the dark corners.

"Welcome," YaYa said from a round table in the middle

of the room. "Sit." She waved her wrinkled hand toward the chair across from her.

In the times I'd visited the encampment, I had only seen her a handful of times. She looked the same, except tonight she wore gold hoop earrings, and a black silk scarf tied around her head. It held back her long silver and black hair. Her hands moved over colorful oversized cards, shuffling them.

Fortune cards...I'd heard of these before.

I gave a slight head nod before sitting. "Good evening."

The older woman waved her hands out. "Your hand, please."

I'd not been nervous until that moment. A brief tremble of trepidation went through me. I'd always been told fortune-telling wasn't real, but after spending the last few weeks with Lily, I now knew better.

Her rough, calloused palm gripped my hands. She turned them over, first the left, then the right. Finally, she ran a crooked index finger along the lines in my palm. About halfway across my hand, her finger stopped. She frowned and then her eyes snapped up.

"What?" Even I heard the note of panic in my voice.

"Toussaint? You in there?" Bernard called out right before the tent flap opened. "Ah, there you are. Lord LaFayette and Lady Marie are asking for you. Come on."

"Toussaint, what're you doing in here?" Pierre followed behind Bernard.

YaYa nodded and sighed, then said something in her native language. Although I didn't understand the words, I understood the look of forlornness when I saw it. Her body sagged in resignation. None of this could be good.

Bernard and Pierre each pulled on an arm and snatched

me out of the seat, but I resisted when they tried to pull me from the tent.

"Wait."

"They want you now," Pierre insisted.

"If they want me that bad, then they can wait one minute." I turned back to YaYa and asked, "What did you see?"

"You will have a very long life." She bundled up her cards, stood, and turned away.

"There," Bernard said as the pair walked me out. "You will grow to be an old man."

I don't know why, but her words left my stomach queasy. Before my friends had burst in, she was about to say more. I was sure of it. At least one thing was certain...in the next few minutes, I would learn more about my immediate future.

When we reached the ballroom, an ethereal voice I knew well filled the room. The men next to me were all but forgotten as the delicate sound lured me to the front of the dais.

Lily.

She was here, and I couldn't talk to her. Bernard and Pierre jostled me as they fell in beside me. Only then did I see how much more packed the ballroom seemed than it had been for the dances. What in the world was the lord going to announce? It must have been important to lure Elder outside of the cigar room. He only attended these for my mother's sake, but this time they both stood front and center.

A sick feeling went through me as I looked at the hopeful faces of mothers and daughters in the room.

No, my father wouldn't.

I told Elder I wasn't going to do this. I refused to marry a girl I didn't love. I took a step back, but Bernard slapped a hand on my shoulder stilling me. He and Pierre took up the space on either side of me.

"What the hell is going on?" Bernard leaned in and whispered.

My mouth went dry. Maybe I was wrong and I did want to speak it into existence. I shook my head instead.

Lord LaFayette chimed a golden bell and the crowd noise lowered to a whisper. Elder's smile widened and he preened more than usual. He looked happy, maybe just a bit too happy.

I wanted to believe they were making him a lord of something at last and he would leave me alone. But looking at his face now, I knew better.

The entertainers stayed behind my cousin as he spoke, to my dismay. Lily stood on the far side of the room. Seeing her sent my thoughts spinning. If Lily were to leave, I would sneak off to talk to her. I longed to kiss her lips and walk proudly with her by my side as my wife. The more I thought about it, the more it sounded right. I would enjoy being married to Lily. We could travel the world, leaving all of this pomp and circumstance behind. If only I could get to her. Nothing my cousin was about to say had anything to do with me, so maybe I could ease over to her now and we could sneak out. Except, she didn't move, and so I soothed myself with watching her beautiful face.

Out of nowhere, her lips tightened, and she looked about the room. What was she searching for?

The lord's voice was a faint nuisance.

Wait. What?

The persistent clapping snapped me out of it. As I looked around, everyone's eyes were on me.

"You sly one. You kept this a big secret," Pierre said as he patted my shoulder.

"Congratulations," Bernard whispered.

What are they talking about?

I had no clue, but then I saw the tears streaming down Lily's face as she ran out of the room. It was clear something had gone terribly wrong.

What just happened? What exactly did my cousin say?

I'd been so caught up in my own fantasies, I'd missed the announcement. When I moved to go after Lily, my father appeared and grabbed my arm in a viselike grip.

"Come along, son," Elder hissed through a fake smile.

"I was just—"

"I know exactly what you were about to do. She's gone. Your future is here. Look around you, boy. Do not embarrass yourself or your family."

I didn't care about me so much, but the bastard knew I loved my mother and sister too much to dishonor them by running out now. Especially with everyone looking.

He led me to a young woman dressed in a soft, flowy, yellow gown which matched her short blond hair. "François, please greet your future bride, Anderly Boniface."

My what? I couldn't have heard him correctly.

My father had sprung his trap. I stared at him, then the young woman. I smiled and her cheeks flushed in a bright hue of pink as her eyes stayed fixed on the floor.

Her parents looked on with pride and there were tears in my mother's eyes. There was no way I could just walk out.

Anderly reached for me first. The softness of her voice required me to lean in to hear her. "It is a pleasure to meet you."

It took a moment for me to remember all of my manners, but then I patted her small hand as it rested on my forearm. "Enchanté."

I had to get through this evening, and then I could fix

this mess. The rest of the evening I walked around with Anderly like a doll pulled by a string. I couldn't wait to have words with my father. For tonight, for this girl's sake and reputation, I smiled and stayed cordial, all while seething inside.

When would this nightmare end?

8

NEW PLAN

$\mathcal{W}$arm sunlight filled the room. Every time I closed my eyes, all I saw was Lily and the tears streaming down her face when my cousin announced my engagement.

My engagement.

Good lord, the sheer thought of this happening the way it had was unfathomable. It all seemed like a bad dream.

After I saw Anderly to her carriage, my friends took me to the club to celebrate my pending nuptials. I don't know what time I awoke, but I watched a spider spin a web in the corner of the sitting room. I would keep that bit of information to myself. If I told my mother she would move us all out of the house until all manner of pests were eradicated.

All night, all I'd wanted to do was go see Lily, but the bourbon kept flowing, and before I knew it, I was too deep in my cups to see straight. There was no way I could see her until I'd sobered up.

"Darling." Mother had come into the room and I hadn't even noticed. "Did you sleep out here all night?" Without letting me respond, she continued, "No matter. You need to get dressed."

My head pounded the moment I sat up and lowered my feet to the floor.

Clap-clap-clap.

Mother's hands sounded like boulders crash landing in my brain, then rolling around inside my skull.

I held my head and whispered, "Mother, please."

"Oh, oh." She lowered her voice and sat next to me. "I will have Marie bring you something for that, but you need to get dressed."

"Why? What's going on?"

She pulled a card from her pocket. "We are having breakfast with the Bonifaces. Your future in-laws." She leaned back and giggled like a young girl.

"I can't."

"You can and you will. Your father worked very hard to find you this match. You will be a baron." Mother squealed in joy. "Isn't that just glorious?"

"Mother, you know that's not what I want." I closed my eyes. "I want to love my wife. If I ever have one."

"You will have a wife. And one day you will love her. Just give it time."

My fingers massaged circles at my temples. My mother wasn't understanding, or was simply not trying to hear me. "I want real love."

She sighed. "You've already found that someone, haven't you?"

I nodded.

My mother continued. "The woman you've been sneaking around with?"

"How did you know?"

"Darling, just because I'm older than you doesn't mean I'm blind."

Quiet stretched out between us, but I had nothing to say. "Is she the one?"

I nodded because I couldn't find the words, but in my heart, I was sure.

"Your father will not be happy about this."

"I know," I said as I stood.

Mother eyed me up and down. "Where are you going?"

"I want to see Lillianna and explain."

"How does she already know?"

"Unfortunately, she was there last night." I tucked my shirt in.

Mother's eyebrow lifted. "Oh, do I know her family?"

I wanted to stop this line of questioning, but couldn't yell nor shake my head. "No, you wouldn't."

"Well, son, you can't go to her looking like that." Mother leaned in and sniffed, then recoiled. "And certainly not smelling like that. You need a bath and a shave. I will send Jean-Luc up to attend you."

"I can do it myself."

"Not if you propose to fix this."

Propose.

When she said the word, my heart pounded until I thought it would burst from my chest. Although she hadn't meant it the same way, I was thinking about it now. Because I loved that woman and her crazy family. I kissed my mother on both cheeks before heading upstairs. If I could convince Lily that last night was a huge misunderstanding, then maybe we could start a new life together.

A new life.

I liked the sound of that.

9

DEATH

*C*old stares greeted me when I entered the campsite later that day. Drova's face lit up as he walked toward me. Before the boy reached me, Pasha grabbed him and turned him away. The boy looked back at me with such sadness in his eyes. Even my most ardent advocate couldn't greet me. This would not be easy.

I knocked on the door of Lily's wagon. I didn't expect her to answer, and she didn't. It surprised me at who did, though.

YaYa stared at me for what felt like a full minute. She *tsked*, then shook her head. "Come, child."

I followed her through the clearing and when I caught up, I said, "I can tell all of you know what happened last night, but—"

She stopped walking without warning and her hand snapped out. "I do not care. Just end it. I love my grand-daughter and I will protect her."

I wanted to say I loved her, too, but YaYa didn't look like she was in the mood to hear anything else from me. Instead, the old woman waved her wrinkled hand toward a round black wagon. "Five minutes."

The three wooden steps creaked under my weight as I neared my future. Almost felt like I was walking to my own death and still I kept walking. I had no choice. Everything in me screamed she was the only one for me. I had no doubts about my love for her.

Lily stood at the far end of the room, arms clenching herself.

"Lily..."

"How could you?" she snapped out. "Was I just a toy to you?"

"Of course not. That girl was my father's choice. *You* are mine."

"If she was his choice, then I will never be yours." She wiped angrily at fresh tears. "I will never be good enough for your family."

"I want to be with you. Only you. It doesn't matter what they think." I moved closer to her, but she evaded my every step, a difficult feat in the small quarters.

"I care. Don't you understand? I care." She sighed, and it held so much finality in it, I worried what her next words would be.

"Please don't—" I began.

"This isn't going to work."

I'd never dreaded hearing five words so much in my life. "Don't do this, Lily."

Before I knew what my own intentions were, I was across the room and Lily was in my arms. She felt so good, I didn't want to let her go.

"Please, don't say that. I—"

Her fingers covered my mouth. I wanted to kiss them,

then keep telling her how much I loved her. I would repeat it until she believed me.

"It's over," she said through tears instead.

Never was all I kept thinking.

Lily tugged against my grip and I couldn't understand why she would give up without fighting for us. I couldn't let her go. Not now. Not ever.

"You're hurting me."

"I would never, but I can't live without you."

"Let me go!" Lily screamed.

"Stay with me..."

None of the other words I wanted to say got out as a piercing pain went through my midsection. I looked down as a red circled blossomed on my pristine white shirt.

I touched the moist spot and my hand came away coated with blood. Then, my gaze met Lily's. "Why?" fell from my lips.

Lily looked at me in horror. I hadn't seen who had stabbed me but could feel myself slipping away from her. As her face went blurry, I surmised this was probably my last chance to tell her.

"I love you."

It seemed like Lily slipped through my fingers after that, but at least the truth was out there. I could die a happy man.

"No!" Lily screamed again. "Drova, what did you do?"

"He was hurting you," Drova cried.

I turned my head to see YaYa pull Drova back and hand him off to a young woman. The older woman pointed and a few pairs of hands turned me on my side. While I could still hear everything around me, it was too much effort to keep my eyes open.

"YaYa, don't let him die. He loves me. This happened because he loves me, and I love him."

I could feel my life slipping away. It didn't matter, though, because she loved me.

"Yes-yes, now get my bag."

Lily's tears fell like a soft rain on my face. My death was breaking her heart. If I could apologize, I would. This would be her last memory of me and I could only lay here and watch her beautiful face.

"Girl!" YaYa yelled. "Go get my bag if you don't want him to die."

Lily's flow of tears stopped and I didn't hear her again before my body was jostled by at least three pairs of hands and moved again. When I forced my eyes open, the old lady was above me, staring down like the dark side of the moon.

"Because she loves you, I will save you, but you will never know genuine love again. You'll never have a family of your own, not until you know the love of a Death Maiden. And pray she doesn't kill you first," she promised.

Lily ran up, out of breath. "Here, YaYa."

The old woman rummaged through a black velvet sack, then poured a powder into her palm, which she quickly blew into my face.

Black dust settled in my eyes, up my nose, and in my mouth, burning me like a torch — inside and out. Moments later, it felt as if all of my insides were ablaze. I would have preferred death if this 'treatment' was supposed to save me. My body convulsed, coming up off the ground then crashing back down. Pain seared through me. In my mind, I thought she was using a knife to filet the skin from my bones. It was more than I could bear and I let go, welcoming death like an old friend.

10

INCUBUS BORN

*W*hen I woke up on the steps of my family's home screaming, there wasn't a spot on me which didn't hurt. My entire body felt like it'd been broken, right down to my smallest toes, and then put back together a little off kilter. My joints popped anytime I moved. My chest tightened when I tried to stand and breathing was a laborious task. As luck would have it, the butler found me and helped me into the house. It took two weeks, maybe a little longer, before I could move without discomfort.

At first, I couldn't remember how I'd ended up like this. The entire night with Lily remained a blur. Until I recalled the blood blossoming at my abdomen, which made it all rush back.

Drova had stabbed me with a thin sword, and I almost died.

No matter how bad off I was, it had to be worse for Lily and Drova. I wanted to let them know I had recovered. That everything was fine between us all. Except, mother watched me like a hawk and me not being able to walk, ensured it didn't happen.

About a month later, I convinced my mother I felt healed enough to ride in the carriage. The damned contraption hit every cobblestone and hole in the road and nearly killed me all over again, but I would never tell anyone. When we reached the campsite, it looked as if no one had ever lived there. Lily and the rest of her nomadic tribe had packed up and left the lavender fields. I knew then I would never see her again. There was no way for them to know if I had survived or not. They'd probably be worried the authorities would come to them looking for the murderer. They had to protect their way of life, family, and Drova, of course.

It was another week before I truly understood what YaYa had done in order to save me. A hunger now ravaged me, but I soon realized it wasn't food that my body craved. I didn't know what to call it or if it even had a name. All I wanted was sex and it occupied my every thought, day and night.

A permanent room at the Turkish bathhouse was reserved for me at some point. I needed sex and copious amounts of it, and of course my parents knew. There wasn't a maid in the house that I hadn't ravished. They'd watched my comings and goings for weeks, and heard the rumors whispered around town. Finally, there was no choice but to call off the marriage to Anderly. Elder put me on a ship and was commanded never to return. Her family was told that I'd died. No one wanted to admit that I'd become a sexual deviant.

The man I had once been had died on the wagon floor that night, and an incubus was born.

11

TODAY

*L*ooking down at the sleeping women I'd exhausted and drained, two tears ran down my face and I didn't wipe them away. It had been a long time since I'd thought about that day, my second birth. For years, I continued to visit the lavender fields, hoping to encounter Lily or her family, but the nomads never returned.

YaYa's promise held true; I had lived and would continue to live for a long time. As of yet, I had not found genuine love or the same true happiness like I had experienced with Lily. Women, however, were drawn to me like a moth to a flame and were burned just as quick.

The old gypsy's curse took many things from me: family, friendships and faith to believe in anything. The true insidiousness of this damnation was how YaYa offered a grain of hope, a way to end this torture. In over three hundred years of immortality, I'd never come across a Death Maiden.

Now, I even doubt their existence.

. . .

The End
Au revoir

AFTERWORD

Thank you for reading **Incubus Born.** I hope you enjoyed Francois' origin story. If you want to find out more about the intriguing incubus, Francois' story continues in Judge,Jury, and Two Exes.

Keep reading for an exclusive excerpt of R.R. Born's
Judge, Jury, and Two Exes
The *FIRST* Death Maiden Chronicles novel!

Still want more stories from the Death Maiden world? Grab Rozlyn's origin story -
Curses and Other Family Secrets

EXCULSIVE EXCERPT FROM JUDGE, JURY, AND TWO EXES

(THIS EXCERPT IS UNEDITED AND UNCORRECTED)

The Thorny Rose had been the primary hub for the supernatural community in New Orleans for more than two centuries. Humans loved the place just as much as the preternaturals. They kept the place packed every weekend and twice as full during Mardi Gras. It might be the drinks or the live music, but dollars to beignets it had something to do with the unnaturally gorgeous men and women that were always in attendance.

The first time Roz came into the bar, she could hardly believe that these people were real. Now, she knew most weren't human. This was one of NOLA's best kept secrets.

Roz and Lester side-stepped the long line and walked in. Lester's broad shoulders and sheer size made people move aside as they walked to the bar. Once they got their drinks, he led her to a back corner table where she could look at the stage and the incoming flow of people. A lot of the customers looked inebriated already, but that didn't stop them from staggering straight to the bar again.

Lester found a booth and sat across from each other. He lifted his beer and Roz clinked her martini glass to his.

"Cheers."

Lester took a healthy swallow before asking, "It's just us two. You want to tell me what's really going on?"

Roz looked down, picking at the lacquer on the tabletop. It seemed to be the most interesting thing suddenly. She shook her head. "Nothing. I'm fine."

The big man hadn't made a sound. She finally looked up through squinted eyes. He frowned, leaned forward, and curled his enormous arms on the table.

Roz rushed to finish before he preached, and he would. "Okay, a few of the ladies from the community." She lifted her fingers to create air quotes for the last word. "Came to inform me that crime was on the rise and it was my fault. Apparently, some supes have been using their powers out in the open."

Lester shook his head. "What the hell?"

"I don't know what I can do about that. Les, I'm not cut out to be this Justice. One person can't police an entire city of supernatural beings. I don't want to see their deepest, darkest, vilest secrets. That shit doesn't magically go away, you know. It stays with me." She tapped her temples.

Lester rubbed his hands on his thighs. "I didn't know, but Rozlyn...your grandmother thought you could do it. She wouldn't have given you this responsibility if she thought you couldn't handle it."

Roz's sad eyes looked at his big brown ones. "I want to believe you. I want to believe Gran knew what she was doing when she gave me this power. But honestly—" She shook her head.

"While you are throwing yourself this pity party, think about this. If you hadn't touched me, I'd still be in the dark about my true nature and I'm not an evil person."

"True, but you were different. You are different," Roz interjected.

"You're right. I was worse. I was a bodyguard...among other things." Lester looked down as he garbled the last part of the sentence. "For the biggest gangster in town."

Roz couldn't say anything to that. Les had kidnapped her when she didn't even know she had powers. She accidentally unbound magic that kept his true nature a secret. Even from himself.

Lester didn't touch her, he knew from past experience no to, but waved his hand in front of her eyes to bring her back to the here and now. "Rozlyn, I can see you're scared. Hell, I know how you feel, but it doesn't stop the fact that we are who we are. No matter how much we try to hide from ourselves."

Her heart ached knowing every word he said was true. There was no way to explain that their situations were completely different. She looked him in the eyes and gave him a tight nod instead. He seemed to take that, as *it was okay*. And it pained her she couldn't tell him it really wasn't.

"Okay," he said enthusiastically.

Roz smiled, then said, "Okay."

She took a long sip from her martini. It was cool on her tongue and when the alcohol hit her system; she knew it. The tension that had held her shoulder like two taut coil springs loosened. She finished the last of the drink. They'd only known each other a few months, but Roz couldn't remember if she ever heard the big man talk this much before. Listening to him now, she felt like she was getting to know the real Lester Broussard.

A drink appeared in front of her. The chilled martini glass glowed with a blue liquid. Roz heard a growl before she looked up to the server who'd delivered the martini. She knew it was a man by the delicious cologne he wore. His scent warmed her to the very core.

"You looked thirsty, *mon amour*," a sultry deep French accent purred. "And I so hate to see a woman wanting."

Roz couldn't believe her eyes. The six foot plus, sandy-haired man was a specimen of male perfection. She wasn't sure what he was, but he was not the type to buy her a drink.

"Go away, man whore," Lester growled.

The beautiful man squinted his lavender eyes in Lester's direction. "No one's talking to you," he sniffed the air, "what is that buffalo, wildebeest?" He wrinkled his nose at Lester, then looked back at Roz. "I'm sure the new Justice can speak for herself."

This man knew what she was. *How?* Roz's hand whipped out in front of Lester to stop him from jumping across the table at the man.

Lester sat back but didn't take his eyes off the visitor. Something came over Roz. She lifted the drink, tilted it towards the visitor in a 'here's to you' salute, then turned up the martini glass like it was a shot of tequila.

"Rozlyn."

She heard Lester admonish, but she held up her other hand to ward off anymore words until she finished the drink.

Roz carefully held the empty glass out to the sexy man in front of her. His pale purple eyes seemed to deepen into amethyst as he laughed. The kind of laugh that rolled down your spine like fingers playing the scale on a piano. She squirmed in her seat, not wanting him to see what kind of affect he was having on her.

"Thank you..." Roz paused as she held his laughing eyes.

"Francois," he said, as he took the waiting glass in one hand, then slid his right hand into her gloved one.

Panic wiped away her bold facade as Roz tried to snatch her hand away. Francois, whatever he was, was also fast. Although she wore gloves, she could feel power roll off him into her palm. She was still new to this, but his power didn't feel malicious. It felt warm and seductive.

"What are you?" Roz breathed out huskily.

A slow smile spread across Francois' face. "You *are* new if you don't know what I am."

"He's a man whore and you don't need to talk to him," Lester said while glaring at the man.

Roz tore her eyes away from Francois, but never releasing his hand. "Now, now Les. Isn't that why you brought me here? To meet new people."

"Not his kind. His kind ain't nothing but trouble," Lester said.

Finally, Roz pulled her hand from his grip, and preceded pulled off her gloves. "I need to know those as well."

"Roz, no. Anyone but him." Lester pleaded.

"It'll be okay. I have a good feeling about this," Roz said, then gave Lester a wink. "Now," she looked up at the devastatingly handsome Francois with her bare hand out. "How do you do? My name is Roz Vincent."

Instead of taking her hand, Francois went to one knee in front of her. It looked like he was ready to propose. Once he bowed his head and closed his eyes, the surrounding voices quieted. Roz only vaguely took stock of what was happening around her, because the man before her was in pain.

Without another thought, Roz's hand cradled his cheek. Her power flowed from him to her. Flashes of a life that began long before television or even electricity. Her other hand found his other cheek, and the circuit was complete. François Henri Toussaint DeChevalier was complicated, complex, harsh, and tender-hearted, and all those things would barely scrape the surface of his true nature.

A seducer of women. A sexual demon. He was literally what wet dreams were made of. François was an incubus.

So much information rushed into her, it overwhelmed all of her senses. The last thing she remembered was leaning forward to kiss his forehead, but he'd lifted his head at the same time. Their lips met, and for once, there was no pain. Roz just wanted to lounge in that feeling for a moment, but when he took control of the kiss, pulling her tongue deeper into his hot mouth. The kiss deepened and she let go of every inhibition. then her world went black.

ACKNOWLEDGMENTS

I'd like to thank everyone who helped this little book get finished. Especially like to thank my editors R.E. Hargrave and Kay Copeland. Thank you for making this story what it is today.

My *Proofreader Extraordinaires*, Ken Wallen and Anesa Michalek. You guys were stiff competition for those ever persistent typos. Thank you.

And to my readers, thank you for taking this journey with me. I still have a lot more stories for you. So get ready, it's going to be a rowdy time in Nawlings.

R.R.

ABOUT THE AUTHOR

R.R. Born is the author of the highly popular, Gray Witch series. She lives in Texas with her husband, and an orange tabby terror named, Pele and a rescued English Bulldog named Joey. She graduated from Houston Community College where she studied Photography, then graduated with a degree in Film and screenwriting from Long Island University in Brookville, NY. She's worked as a Production Coordinator, Second Assistant Director on local commercials, TLC & HGTV shows, and movies.

For more info on upcoming projects, sign up for my Newsletter
www.rrborn.com

ALSO BY R.R. BORN